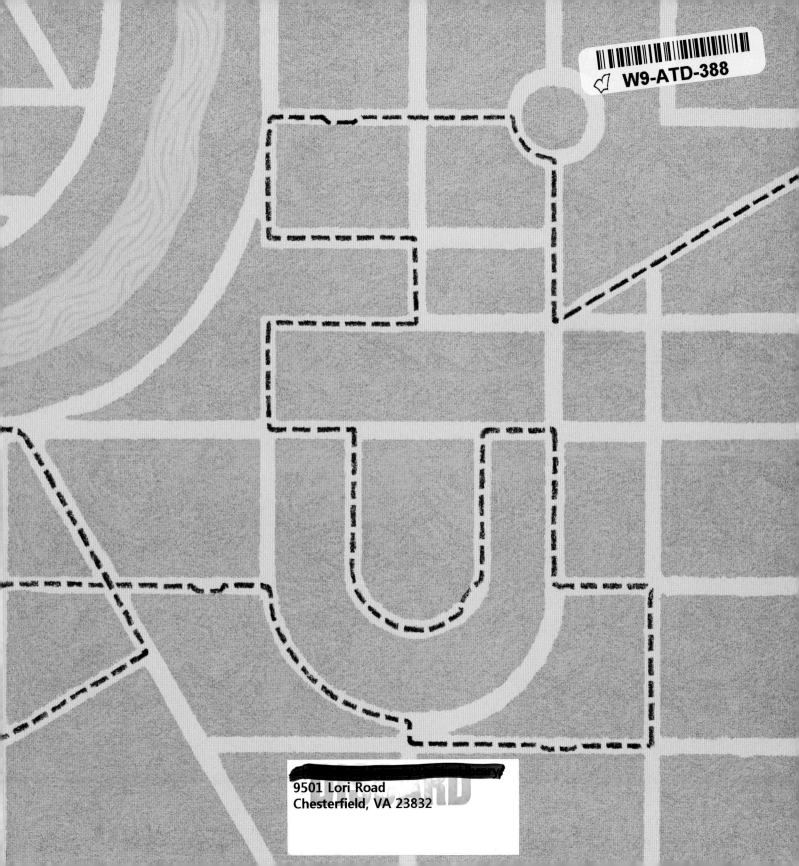

W9-ATD-388

When my brother gets home

TOM LICHTENHELD

Houghton Mifflin Harcourt | Boston • New York

When my brother gets home . . .

we're going to have
after-school snacks . . .

for the entire kingdom!

When my brother gets home . . .

we're going to have our own
comic book convention.

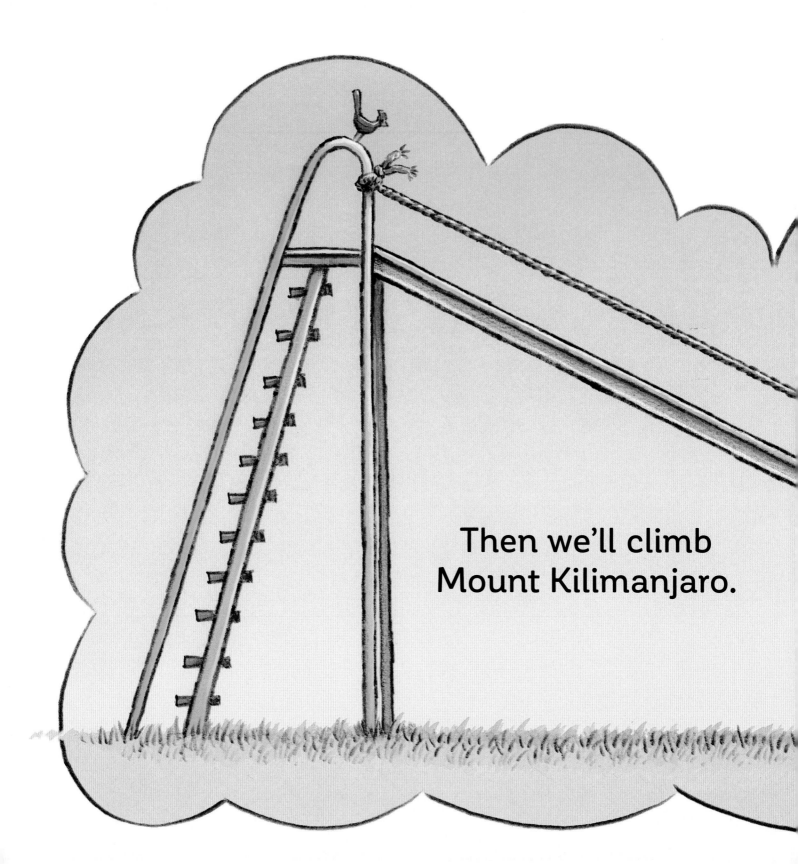

Then we'll climb
Mount Kilimanjaro.

When my brother gets home . . .

we're going to practice
our Olympic dives . . .

venture into the deep,
unexplored rainforest . . .

and build the biggest castle
in the neighborhood.

When my brother gets home . . .

we're going to jump into a waterfall . . .

wrestle an alligator . . .

then fly around the world
in our jumbo jet.

When my brother gets home . . .

I have a MILLION ideas!

hmhbooks.com

The illustrations in this book were done in pencil, watercolor,
and colored pencil on Mi-Teintes paper. Digital enhancement by Kristen Cella.
The text type was set in Corporative Soft Medium.
The display type was set in Mr Eaves Italic.

Library of Congress Cataloging-in-Publication Data
Names: Lichtenheld, Tom, author, Illustrator.
Title: When my brother gets home / Tom Lichtenheld.
Description: Boston ; New York : Houghton Mifflin Harcourt, [2020] |
Summary: A girl imagines amazing adventures she will have when her brother arrives home.
Identifiers: LCCN 2019017580 | ISBN 9781328498052 (hardcover picture book)
Subjects: | CYAC: Brothers—Fiction. | Imagination—Fiction.
Classification: LCC PZ7.L592 Whe 2020 | DDC [E]—dc23
LC record available at https://lccn.loc.gov/2019017580

Manufactured in China
SCP 10 9 8 7 6 5 4 3 2 1
4500785372

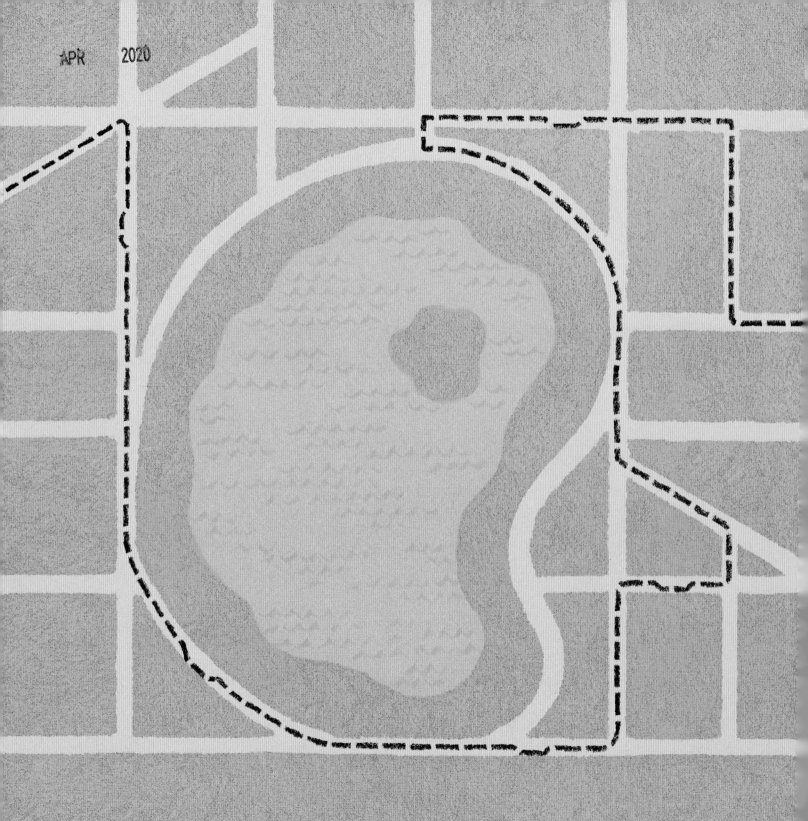